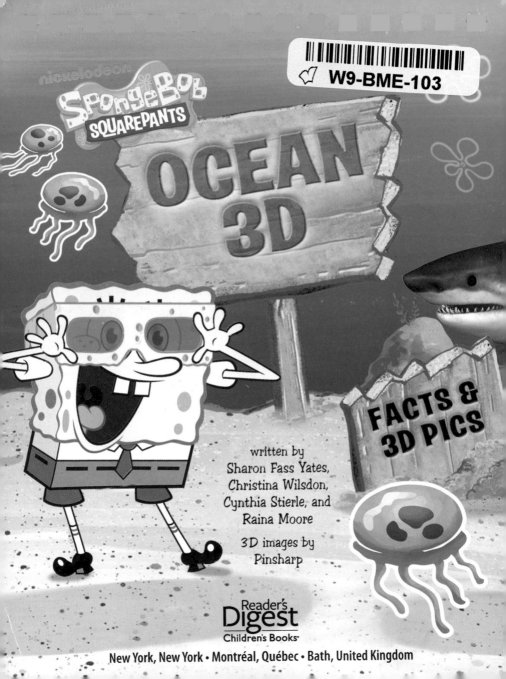

nickelodeon

SpongeBob SQUAREPANTS

OCEAN 3D

FACTS & 3D PICS

written by
Sharon Fass Yates,
Christina Wilsdon,
Cynthia Stierle, and
Raina Moore

3D images by
Pinsharp

Reader's Digest Children's Books

New York, New York • Montréal, Québec • Bath, United Kingdom

CORAL REEF

Welcome to the coral reef! In this remarkable place, there live bright blue sea stars, giant clams, mysterious moray eels, and thousands of fish in every color of the rainbow! Almost a quarter of all the ocean's creatures live in these amazing places—but just what are they?

Before there's a reef, there are coral polyps. These tiny animals live in large groups known as colonies. Each polyp makes a hard tube (its skeleton) and lives inside it. When a polyp dies, the skeleton remains. That brightly colored, tube-like skeleton is called coral.

Over thousands of years, coral polyps can build a reef large enough for other animals to live in—anemones, tubeworms, and, of course, the lovable sponge!

Coral reefs are usually found just offshore in warm tropical water where they look a lot like vibrant, underwater gardens. Some coral resembles trees or flowers while others look like spirals or brains!

So put on your 3D glasses and join our friends from Bikini Bottom and get to know some of the creatures that make the coral reef their home!

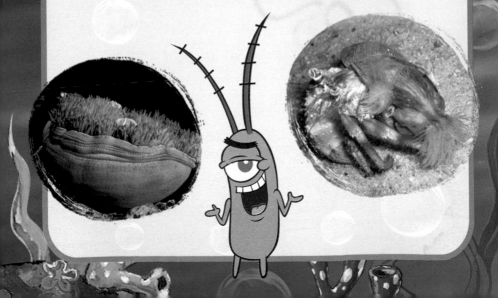

ANEMONEFISH

Food: Algae, zooplankton, scraps from anemones' meals.

Where found: Red Sea and tropical waters of the Indian and western Pacific oceans.

Fun fact: There are about 30 different kinds of anemonefish.

Anemonefish are often called clownfish. Many kinds of anemonefish live among the tentacles of certain sea anemones. The slimy coating of mucus on an anemonefish protects it from getting stung by the anemone's tentacles. Maybe SpongeBob and Patrick should cover themselves in mucus when they're jellyfishing!

ANEMONE HERMIT CRAB

Food: Fish, snails, worms, algae, dead animals.

Where found: Tropical waters of the western Pacific Ocean.

Fun fact: The hermit crab often plucks the anemones off its old shell and puts them on its new one.

A hermit crab tucks its soft body into a discarded shell and hangs on with a few of its hind legs. As it grows, it gets rid of old shells and finds bigger ones. Too bad Squidward can't get a bigger house far away from SpongeBob! This species is called the anemone hermit crab because it carries stinging anemones on its shell for extra protection.

You live in a shell.
I live under a rock.
Shell, rock, shell, rock.
Whew, I'm tired.

FOUR-EYED BUTTERFLYFISH

Food: Coral polyps, sea fans, marine worms, sea squirts.

Where found: Caribbean Sea, Gulf of Mexico, and tropical western Atlantic Ocean.

Fun fact: There are about 115 different kinds of butterflyfish.

A four-eyed butterflyfish looks like it has four eyes, thanks to the two big "eyespots" that peer from its tail end. Eyespots trick a predator into attacking the fish's tail instead of its head. The predator gets a surprise when the butterflyfish zips off in the opposite direction! Plankton could try this trick. But he only has one eye—mmmm.

BLUE SEA STAR

Food: Algae and dead animals.

Where found: Tropical waters of the Indian and western and central Pacific oceans.

Size: About 12 inches wide when fully grown.

Fun fact: The blue sea star has hundreds of yellow tube-shaped feet on its underside.

The blue sea star is usually bright blue when it grows up, but some blue sea stars can be pink, yellow, orange, purple, or green! If Pearl had it her way, she'd have twice as many wardrobe options! Tiny shrimp and snails sometimes live in the grooves of a blue sea star's arms. They are blue, too.

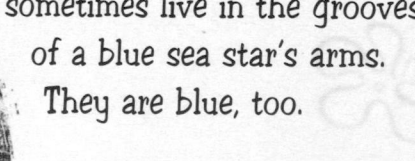

I, too, know what it's like to always get the star treatment.

CHAMBERED NAUTILUS

Food: Fish, crabs, shrimp, dead animals.

Where found: Tropical waters of the western Pacific Ocean.

Fun fact: The chambered nautilus has about 90 arms!

The chambered nautilus is related to octopuses, squid, and cuttlefish. Unlike them, it lives in a shell up to 10 inches wide. By day it sinks deep underwater into the dark zone. At night it swims up to feed closer to the surface. It sniffs out and catches its food with its many arms. But if it ever comes to the Krusty Krab, it'll have to pay for its meals just like everybody else!

CHRISTMAS TREE WORM

Food: Plankton.

Where found: On coral reefs in tropical waters all over the world.

Fun fact: Christmas tree worms are also called feather-duster worms.

The Christmas tree worm is named after the two fluffy "trees" that stick out of its mouth, which are used to filter food from the water and for breathing. The industrious worm drills itself a hole in the coral reef then lives there just like handy Sandy built herself a Treedome to live underwater!

Do Christmas tree worms
get presents all year long?
That's so coral!

BLUESTREAK CLEANER WRASSE

Food: Parasites and dead skin picked from other fish.

Where found: Red Sea and coral reefs in the Atlantic, Pacific, and Indian oceans.

Fun fact: A kind of fish called the false cleaner fish looks like a cleaner wrasse. It fools fish into thinking it is a cleaner but it takes a bite out of them instead!

There are about 300 kinds of wrasses, but the best known are the cleaner wrasses. These little fish set up "cleaning stations" on a reef. They wiggle and squirm to attract big fish. The big fish stay still and let cleaner wrasses nibble pests and bits of dead skin off them. Squidward hopes someone will show Patrick where the cleaning station is!

BROADCLUB CUTTLEFISH

Food: Clams, crabs, shrimp, fish.

Where found: Indian and western and central Pacific oceans.

Size: About 18 inches long.

Fun fact: Broadclub cuttlefish seem to use color changes to dazzle their prey, making them stay still long enough to catch.

Cuttlefish are related to squid and octopuses. The broadclub cuttlefish is one of the largest kinds of cuttlefish. It can change color to help it hunt, scare off predators, find a mate, or hide. It catches prey with its two long tentacles and eight arms. Now if it could use those arms to flip Krabby Patties, it might be of some use to Mr. Krabs!

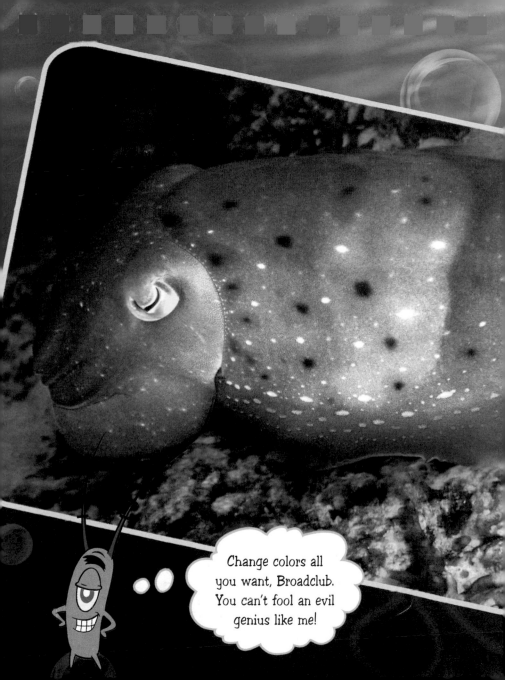

LAGOON TRIGGERFISH

Food: Fish, sea urchins, corals, worms, shrimp.

Where found: Red Sea and tropical waters of the Indian and western and central Pacific oceans.

Fun fact: This fish is also called the Picasso triggerfish. Picasso was a painter (like Squidward) who is now famous (not like Squidward). The lagoon triggerfish's colorful markings look like they were dabbed on with a paintbrush and that's how it got its nickname.

The lagoon triggerfish has spines on its back that are usually folded flat. It raises them after it goes into a hole in a reef. This helps the fish lock itself in place so that it can't be pulled out by a predator. Raised spines also make a triggerfish hard to swallow.

GIANT CLAM

Food: Plankton filtered from water, food made by algae.

Where found: Red Sea and tropical waters of the Indian and western Pacific oceans.

Fun fact: A giant clam can live for more than 100 years.

The giant clam can grow to be 4 feet long (longer than a yardstick) and can weigh as much as 500 pounds! Algae living in the giant clam's body provide food for the clam in exchange for a safe place to live. Clams and algae live together in harmony—just like SpongeBob and Gary!

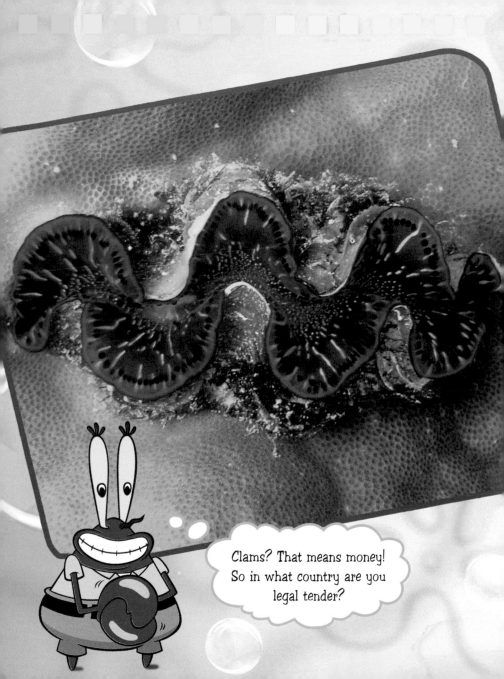

DAY OCTOPUS

Food: Crabs, small fish, shrimp, clams.

Where found: Red Sea and the Indian and western and central Pacific oceans.

Fun fact: A day octopus can change its color pattern 1,000 times in just 7 hours.

Many octopuses hunt for food at night to avoid predators—but not the day octopus. This species can change the color and texture of its skin in just seconds as it travels across a reef. That's faster than it takes Mrs. Puff to puff! The nonstop color changes help the day octopus to blend in with its surroundings. It rests in a hole that it burrows in the reef.

PARROTFISH

Food: Coral polyps and algae inside the polyps.

Where found: Red Sea and coral reefs in the Atlantic, Pacific, and Indian oceans.

Fun fact: There are about 80 different kinds of parrotfish, but none of them can talk!

Parrotfish are named for their bright colors and beaklike mouths. The "beak" is really a row of tough teeth that the fish uses for chomping on hard chunks of coral to feed on the soft polyps inside. Some kinds of parrotfish make big clear sacks of mucus and sleep inside them at night. Their slimy "sleeping bags" protect them from predators.

So is your best friend a piratefish?

SCRAMBLED EGG NUDIBRANCH

Food: Sponges.

Where found: Red Sea and tropical waters of the Indian and western and central Pacific oceans.

Fun fact: This sea slug is named for the golden yellow markings on its body. It can grow to be 3 ½ inches long—and miniscule Plankton thinks that is VERY unfair!

A nudibranch is also called a sea slug. The scrambled egg nudibranch eats poisonous sponges. It isn't harmed by the poison. Instead, it stores the poison in its body and uses it to make a smelly, poisonous mucus to protect itself. The mucus kills fish that try to eat it.

SCARLET CLEANER SHRIMP

Food: Parasites and bits of dead skin picked from fish.

Where found: Red Sea and tropical waters of the Indian and western and central Pacific oceans.

Fun fact: The scarlet cleaner shrimp is sometimes called the Indo-Pacific white-striped cleaner shrimp—a long name for a 2-inch animal!

This shrimp defends a patch of coral reef that is its "cleaning station." Fish visit the shrimp to let it pick parasites and bits of dead skin from their bodies and even from inside their mouths! Maybe that sounds strange, but SpongeBob would do the same for Gary!

Impeccable cleaning habits is a sign of impeccably good taste.

LIONFISH

Food: Shrimp, crabs, small fish.

Where found: Red Sea, Indian Ocean, western and central Pacific Ocean, Caribbean Sea, and warm waters of the western Atlantic Ocean.

Fun fact: Lionfish are sometimes called turkeyfish, dragonfish, or zebrafish. Patrick is sometimes called Patrick, Patrick Star, Mr. Star, and "Hey you, give me back that sandwich!"

A lionfish's fins contain a kind of poison called venom. This venom can kill predators such as other fish. The sting is not deadly to a human, but it is very painful. A lionfish confronts a predator by spreading its fins wide.

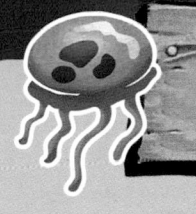

MAGNIFICENT SEA ANEMONE

Food: Fish, shrimp.

Where found: Red Sea and coral reefs in the Indian and western and central Pacific oceans.

Fun fact: This anemone's tentacles stick out of a barrellike column. It can pull its tentacles into the column so that it looks like a big beach ball which is perfect for a trip to Goo Lagoon!

A magnificent sea anemone can grow to be 3 feet wide. It feeds by stinging fish and other 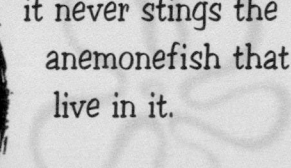 animals with the tentacles that surround its mouth. But it never stings the anemonefish that live in it.

VIOLET SEA CUCUMBER

Food: Algae, plankton, waste products, dead animals.

Where found: Indian and the western Pacific oceans.

Fun fact: There are about 1,250 different kinds of sea cucumbers but there's only one SpongeBob SquarePants!

Sea cucumbers are sausage-shaped relatives of sea stars. A sea cucumber has a soft body lined with tube-shaped feet. Sticky tentacles surround its mouth. It gathers bits of food from water, sand, or mud. The violet sea cucumber is also called a sea apple!

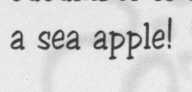

I like your hat,
madame.

GREEN MORAY

Food: Fish, squid, octopuses, crabs.

Where found: Western Atlantic Ocean.

Fun fact: The green moray can grow to almost 8 feet long.

The green moray is an eel that stays near reefs but is also found along rocky shores. It hunts at night using its keen sense of smell. A moray swims by rippling its powerful body—even Larry the Lobster can't do that! The moray can swim backward and forward. About 80 kinds of morays swim in the world's oceans.

Great barrier reef! You are one far-reaching fish!

OPEN WATER

More than 70% of our planet is covered in water, and most of that water is found in the world's five oceans: Atlantic, Pacific, Indian, Southern, and Arctic. More than 200,000 kinds of animals, plants, and one-celled creatures call these vast bodies of water home.

Far from shore, past the coral reefs, are the ocean's wide-open spaces. This is where you'll find the world's largest living animal in history: the blue whale. It is almost 100 feet long! It is also where you will find plankton: a layer of tiny, often microscopic, living plants and animals that float near the water's surface.

Most ocean creatures live within the top 600 feet of water—where sunlight can reach. This is where most

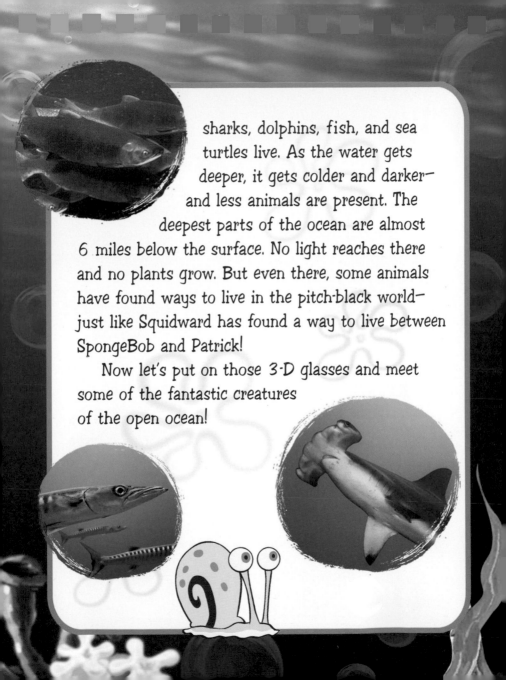

sharks, dolphins, fish, and sea turtles live. As the water gets deeper, it gets colder and darker—and less animals are present. The deepest parts of the ocean are almost 6 miles below the surface. No light reaches there and no plants grow. But even there, some animals have found ways to live in the pitch-black world—just like Squidward has found a way to live between SpongeBob and Patrick!

Now let's put on those 3-D glasses and meet some of the fantastic creatures of the open ocean!

ATLANTIC MACKEREL

Food: Zooplankton, fish, shellfish.

Where found: North Atlantic Ocean, Mediterranean Sea.

Size: 1-2 feet long.

Fun fact: Sometimes called a striped mackerel, this fish has wavy lines that run across the top half of its body.

Mackerel have a streamlined shape which helps make them fast swimmers. They travel in large schools, sometimes for thousands of miles, to feed or reproduce. Sandy traveled like a mackerel thousands of miles from Texas to live in Bikini Bottom!

BLUEFIN TUNA

Food: Fish, shellfish.

Where found: Warm and temperate areas of the Atlantic Ocean, Mediterranean Sea, Black Sea, and eastern Pacific Ocean.

Size: Up to 12 feet long and 1,500 pounds.

Bluefins are the giants of the tuna world in the same way that SpongeBob is a giant in the patty flipping world. Okay, so bluefins are bigger—they can grow to be 1,500 pounds! But many are caught in high-tech fishing nets before they reach their full size. In fact, bluefins are so highly prized by sport fishermen and commercial fisheries that many people believe these fish will soon be an endangered species.

GREAT BARRACUDA

Food: Fish, squid, octopuses.

Where found: Tropical oceans, but not the eastern Pacific Ocean.

Size: About 5 feet long and 100 pounds.

Fun fact: Despite their fierce reputations, barracudas do not usually attack humans unless the humans have annoyed them.

The long, sleek barracuda has a big mouth and very sharp teeth that help it attack and eat large prey. It often waits for its prey to get within range and then swims very fast to pounce on it. Barracudas usually swim alone, but in wintertime, schools of barracudas have been sighted. And a few times a year, SpongeBob has been sighted in boating school. Okay, all year.

SOCKEYE SALMON

Food: Zooplankton, small fish.

Where found: North Pacific Ocean, Arctic Ocean, and the rivers that flow into them.

Size: Up to 3 feet long.

Born in rivers, sockeyes swim to the ocean when still young and live there for about two years. Then they return to the very same rivers they came from to produce baby sockeyes. In the ocean, sockeyes are silver-colored. Back in their river birthplaces, they become red, with green heads and tails. Mr. Krabs becomes red when he's steamed! Hahaha. Steamed, angry!

LEATHERBACK TURTLE

Food: Jellyfish, fish, shellfish.

Where found: Usually temperate and warm areas of oceans but also colder areas, too.

Size: Nearly 7 feet long, about 1,600 pounds.

Fun fact: A female leatherback lays about 100 eggs and then covers them with sand to keep them hidden and safe until they hatch. Patrick covers himself with a rock but he still hasn't matured!

The leatherback is the world's largest turtle. It is named for its soft, leathery shell. A hard shell would be crushed by the force and weight of the ocean water. Female leatherbacks come ashore every two or three years to make nests in the sand and lay their eggs. Then they return to the ocean.

PORTUGUESE MAN-OF-WAR

Food: Mostly young and small fish, plankton.

Where found: Anywhere in the open ocean—especially the tropical regions.

Size: Body up to 12 inches long, tentacles up to 33 feet long.

Fun fact: The balloonlike top faces to the right on some Portuguese man-of-wars and to the left on others because the wind blows them in opposite directions.

The Portuguese man-of-war bobs along on or near the water's surface. It goes wherever the wind or currents take it just like Patrick's train of thought! Its balloonlike top acts as a float. Don't step on a dead man-of-war—the stinging cells on its long, curly tentacles can still give you a painful stab!

BLUESPOTTED RIBBONTAIL RAY

Food: Mollusks, worms, crustaceans.

Where found: Indo-Pacific oceans.

Size: About 2½ feet long, and 14 inches across.

Fun fact: These rays are sometimes cleaned by tiny fish or shrimp that pick and eat dead skin off their backs. Mermaidman wishes BarnacleBoy would pick off his dead skin! But that's another story...

Unlike most rays, the bluespotted ribbontail ray doesn't usually bury itself in the sand. But its bright colors may warn predators to stay away, since the spines on the ray's tail can deliver a poisonous and painful sting.

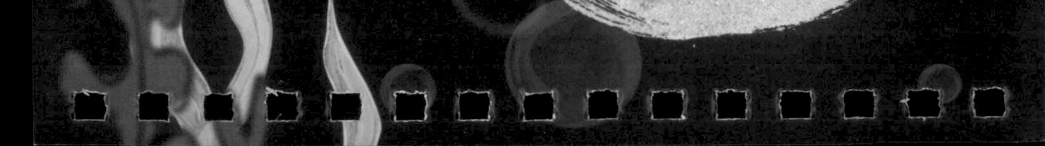

GREAT
HAMMERHEAD SHARK

Food: Seals, sea lions, sea turtles, carcasses of whales.

Where found: Cooler coastal waters, including the Atlantic, Pacific, and Indian oceans.

Size: 10-20 feet long, 500-1,000 pounds.

The largest of the hammerhead species, this shark uses its unusually shaped head to catch and eat stingrays. And Mr. Krabs uses his unusually shaped head to make money! Immune to the ray's stings, the shark pins the ray down on the ocean floor with one side of its head and then takes bites out of the ray's fins.

BLACKTIP REEF SHARK

Food: Reef fish, crustaceans, snakes.

Where found: Coastal waters in the Indian and western Pacific oceans.

Size: Up to 7 feet long and 30 pounds.

Fun fact: Some blacktip reef sharks near Australia eat sea snakes.

Divers exploring the coral reefs are likely to spot one of these sharks swimming along with them in the shallow coastal waters. Sometimes these sharks swim together in a group, herding a school of fish into a tight ball. Then the sharks dart through the ball of fish to feed. They could just go to the grocery store for a box of Kelpo. Unlike schools of fish, Kelpo comes with a free prize offer!

GREAT WHITE SHARK

Food: Seals, sea lions, sea turtles, carcasses of whales.

Where found: Cooler coastal waters, including the Atlantic, Pacific, and Indian oceans.

Size: 10-15 feet long, 2,500-3,000 pounds (can be up to 23 feet long and 4,000 pounds).

Fun fact: The great white's tremendous mouth is full of teeth—up to 300 of them lined up in several rows.

The great white is the only shark that can lift its head out of the water to look for its dinner. But it usually relies on its amazing sense of smell and its ability to sense electrical charges to find its prey. Patrick just relies on his stomach to point in the direction of the nearest Krabby Patty.

SPOTTED EAGLE RAY

Food: Mollusks, crustaceans, sea urchins, small bony fish.

Where found: Worldwide in warm, temperate, and tropical coastal waters.

Size: About 8 feet wide, up to 500 pounds.

Just like Squidward Tentacles performing his original modern dance, this graceful creature appears to "fly" under the water as it beats its large fins up and down. But it can also leap out of the water when it is being chased by a predator such as a hammerhead shark— and then it looks as if it's flying for real.

WHALE SHARK

Food: Tiny plant and animal plankton, schools of small fish.

Where found: Tropical and temperate oceans worldwide, usually near the water's surface.

Size: Up to 45 feet long and 13 tons.

Fun fact: Despite its huge size, the whale shark isn't dangerous to people or sponges in clean underwear!

The whale shark is the largest fish in all the world's oceans—it's about the size of a school bus. But this shark feeds on some of the ocean's tiniest creatures. Even though it has thousands of teeth in its huge mouth, the whale shark is a "filter feeder." It strains food from the water by forcing the water over filter pads in its gills.

Spending time with a hungry shark couldn't be any worse that spending time with GrinningBob ShrillPants.

BELUGA WHALE

Food: Squid, fish, shellfish, sea worms.

Where found: Arctic Ocean and nearby seas.

Size: 13-14 feet long, up to 2,600 pounds (females); 14-16 feet long, up to 3,500 pounds (males).

Fun Fact: A baby beluga is born with dark gray skin that, as it grows older, turns white as the hair on Mermaidman's head!

Belugas make many high-pitched squeaks, whistles, and chirps, which led early sailors to call them "sea canaries." Belugas can swim on their backs, using their tail flukes as paddles.

HUMPBACK WHALE

Food: About 1 ½ tons a day of krill, herring, and other small fish.

Where found: All the oceans of the world.

Size: About 50 feet long, up to 40 tons (females a bit larger than males).

Humpbacks are famous for the long and complicated songs that the males sing underwater. And Pearl Krabs is famous for long and complicated trips to the mall! Each group of humpback males living in an area sings its own special song. The white markings on the underside of a humpback's tail are unique to each individual whale.

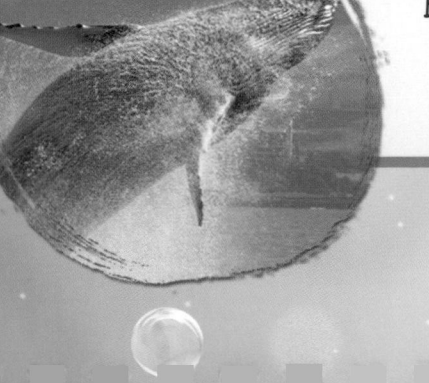

KILLER WHALE

Food: Sea lions, harbor seals, sharks, squid, penguins, smaller whales, fish.

Where found: All the oceans of the world.

Size: Up to 23 feet long and 4 tons (females); up to 32 feet long and 9 tons (males).

Although the killer whale (also called an orca), with its scary-looking dorsal fin sticking up out of the water, is an excellent hunter, it doesn't attack humans in the wild. Killer whales often jump out of the water and belly flop onto the surface with a huge splash. This action is called breaching. Mr. Krabs has a photo of Pearl's first breach in his office.

COMMON BOTTLENOSE DOLPHIN

Food: Fish, squid, snails, other marine animals without backbones.

Where found: Warm regions of the Atlantic and Pacific oceans.

Size: Up to 12½ feet long; up to 570 pounds (females) and over 1,000 pounds (males).

This star performer is the type of dolphin you see doing tricks in movies and aquariums. Mr. Krabs would do tricks in a movie, too. For the right price! It can remember commands and routines. The common bottlenose is very friendly and talks to other dolphins using chirps and whistles.

Oh, what a lovely sound is that of a dolphin laughing!

WEST INDIAN MANATEE

Food: Water plants.

Where found: Coastal waters from southeast United States to Brazil, in South America.

Size: Up to 14 feet long and 3,000 pounds.

Unlike most marine mammals, this manatee can live in both seawater (salty) and fresh water (not salty) habitats. And unlike most squirrels, Sandy can live on land (Texas) or underwater (Bikini Bottom)—with the right equipment of course! Despite its clumsy appearance, the gentle manatee moves easily in water, swimming on its back and doing somersaults.

BIRDS & BEASTS OF THE SEA

Fish aren't the only animals that need the ocean to survive. There are many birds and animals that live on or near the oceans of the world and depend on it for food. They are all well-equipped for life on the water.

Gulls, puffins, terns, and other sea birds spend much of their lives flying over the ocean and feeding from it. Some visit land only to lay eggs and raise their young. Many seabirds have huge wings that help them soar for long stretches at a time. One of the largest wingspans belongs to the albatross. Its wings can stretch more than 10 feet across!

Some birds and mammals spend much of their time under the water.

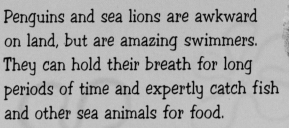

Penguins and sea lions are awkward on land, but are amazing swimmers. They can hold their breath for long periods of time and expertly catch fish and other sea animals for food.

Polar bears, the largest meat-eaters on earth, spend most of their lives in the freezing water of the Arctic hunting seals. Some bears have been found on sheets of ice hundreds of miles from shore. Let's learn more about some of these fascinating animals with SpongeBob!

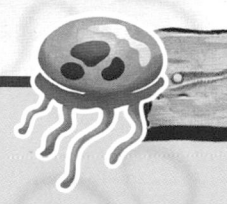

SEA OTTER

Food: Abalone, lobsters, sea urchins, clams.

Where found: Pacific Coast of North America and the Bering Sea, from Siberia to northern Japan.

Size: Up to 5 feet long and 100 pounds.

This cute-as-Gary, furry little creature is the smallest marine mammal. A sea otter often swims on its back on the surface of the water, kicking with its flipper-shaped hind feet. It places food on its chest and belly, using its body as a table. That way, it doesn't have to pay to eat at the Krusty Krab!

NORTHERN ELEPHANT SEAL

Food: Fish, squid.

Where found: Pacific Coast of North America.

Size: About 10 feet long and 1,300 pounds (females); about 13 ½ feet long and 4,400 pounds (males).

Fun fact: While on land, elephant seals snuggle up to one another even when there is plenty of room on the beach to spread out.

When two male elephant seals fight, they inflate their snouts with air to roar as loudly as possible. Just like a good old fashioned Trenchbilly yodling contest, the loudest one wins.

Y'all are snuggled closer than a pot of beans at a barbecue!

CALIFORNIA SEA LION

Food: Anchovies, sardines, mackerel, squid.

Where found: Pacific Coast of North America.

Size: About 7 feet long and 240 pounds (females); about 8 feet long and 860 pounds (males).

As playful and intelligent as Sandra Olivia Cheeks, California sea lions are usually the "seals" you see performing in circuses, zoos, and aquariums. Unlike seals, they can turn their flippers forward and walk on land. They often live in groups and love to bask on rocks, "barking" to one another.

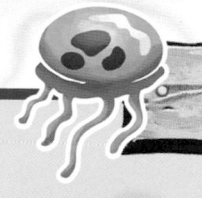

POLAR BEAR

Food: Seals, walruses.

Where found: Arctic Ocean, coasts of Alaska and northern Canada.

Size: Up to 8 feet long and 880 pounds (females); up to 10 feet long and 1,500 pounds (males). In other words, there's no need to make this guy mad!

Polar bears are the biggest bears and the only bears with blubber, a thick layer of fat under the skin that keeps them warm. The pads on their paws have tiny bumps that help stop the bears from sliding on ice.

I have a deep respect for your girth and heft.

BROWN PELICAN

Food: Fish, some types of shrimp.

Where found: East and west coasts of North America and South America.

Size: 42-54 inches long.

A spectacular diver, the brown pelican streaks down through the air with its long beak pointing straight at the ocean. It plunges underwater and rises to the surface just two seconds later with a fish—and water—in its beak. Two seconds to make dinner? Watch out, this guy might try to take SpongeBob's job!

ATLANTIC PUFFIN

Food: Small fish, shrimp, and other shellfish.

Where found: Eastern coast of North America, from Canada to Maine; western coast of Europe, south to England and France.

Size: About 12 inches long.

The puffin is one of the very few birds that can hold many fish in its beak at the same time—just like Patrick can hold many, many, many Krabby Patties in his mouth at the same time! If it doesn't catch a fish after a dive, the puffin chases it by using its wings like paddles to "fly" underwater.

EMPEROR PENGUIN

Food: Fish, squid.

Where found: Coast of Antarctica.

Size: 36-48 inches tall.

The emperor penguin is a bird, but it can't fly. Like other penguins, it uses its wings as flippers for swimming and diving underwater. It can dive 1,500 feet deep—about the distance of a 150-story building! And that little factoid even impresses Sandy, Texan scientist!

JACKASS PENGUIN

Food: Fish, squid, shellfish.

Where found: Coast of southern Africa.

Size: About 27 inches tall.

This penguin got its name not because it acts foolish but because it makes a loud braying noise that sounds like the hee-haw of a donkey. It also goes by two other names: the African penguin and the black-footed penguin. If it were up to Mr. Krabs, all those different names would cost extra.

BLACK-FOOTED ALBATROSS

Food: Fish, squid, shellfish.

Where found: Coasts of the North Pacific Ocean along North America and Asia.

Size: 27-29 inches long.

This big bird looks even bigger when its wings are spread open to nearly seven feet. The wings move up and down stiffly, rather than in graceful flaps, which adds to the bird's threatening appearance. When it floats on the water with its wings tucked in, it looks less scary—sort of like when sneaky Plankton winds up getting squished on the floor!

Time really does fly when you're having fun! It looks like our little trip is over, Mr. Albatross. See you next time!

PHOTO CREDITS